D0684177

Dear Friends,
Some of you may have
noticed that my purple
pen has run out.
But I'm still writing
in my journal!
Love, Abby

The AMAZING DAYS ® of ABBY HAYES

Everything New Under the Sun

Read more books about me!

The AMAZING DAYS® of ABBY HAYES

Everything New Under the Sun

ANNE MAZER

AN
APPLE
PAPERBACK

SCHOLASTIC INC.
New York Toronto London Auckland Sydney
Mexico City New Delhi Hong Kong Buenos Aires

To Madeline
Somebody New Under The Sun

If you purchased this book without a cover, you should be aware that this book is stolen property. It was reported as "unsold and destroyed" to the publisher, and neither the author nor the publisher has received any payment for this "stripped book."

No part of this publication may be reproduced in whole or in part, or stored in a retrieval system, or transmitted in any form or by any means, electronic, mechanical, photocopying, recording, or otherwise, without written permission of the publisher. For information regarding permission, write to Scholastic Inc., Attention: Permissions Department, 557 Broadway, New York, NY 10012.

ISBN 0-439-35369-6

Text copyright © 2003 by Anne Mazer. All rights reserved. Published by Scholastic Inc. SCHOLASTIC, APPLE PAPERBACKS, THE AMAZING DAYS OF ABBY HAYES, and associated logos are trademarks and/or registered trademarks of Scholastic Inc.

Illustrations by Monica Gesue

12 11 10 9 8   6 7 8/0

Printed in the U.S.A.   40

First printing, April 2003

Chapter 1

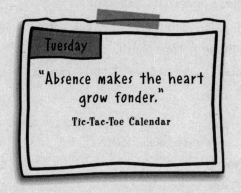

Tuesday

"Absence makes the heart grow fonder."

Tic-Tac-Toe Calendar

Does it?

Case #1

Abby's best friend, Jessica, has been absent for three months. She is in Oregon visiting her father and his new wife and her two stepsisters, Danielle and Dakota.

Has Jessica's absence made her heart grow fonder of Abby?

<u>What Jessica loved before she went away</u>:
1. Drawing
2. Astronomy

3. Math and science
4. Jokes, overalls, striped T-shirts, smiley face buttons
5. Spending time with best friend, Abby, and other best friend, Natalie

What Jessica loves now:
1. Boys
2. Parties
3. Glitter and face paint
4. Dances
5. Spending time with Danielle and her friends

How often Abby hears from Jessica:
Once in a while

How often Jessica says she misses Abby:
Almost never

How often Jessica says she loves staying with her dad and his new family:
All the time — when I get to talk to her

She is going to stay in Oregon until the

end of the school year!!! (She didn't even tell me herself. Jessica's mother called us and told Dad the news.)

Conclusion:
Absence has made Jessica's heart grow forgetful! She has even changed her name to Jessy!

Case #2
Has Jessica's absence made Abby's heart grow fonder?

What Abby misses:
1. Having a best friend to talk to whenever I'm upset or sad or happy or surprised
2. Having sleepovers with my best friend
3. Telling secrets to my best friend

4. Going biking and Rollerblading with my best friend
5. Having a best friend to help me with my math homework

Will I be able to tell secrets to Jessy?

Will she want to go biking with me? Will she help me with my math homework?

Or will she giggle about boys, show me her jars of face glitter, and talk about dances and parties nonstop?

<u>Who Abby misses</u>:
1. The old Jessica

<u>Who Abby doesn't miss</u>:
1. The new Jessy

<u>Conclusion</u>:
Absence has made Abby's heart grow confused! Which one is the <u>real</u> Jessica? How can my heart grow fonder of someone I don't even know anymore?

P.S. My birthday is coming up. How can I celebrate it without a best friend?

Ms. Kantor, Abby's fifth-grade teacher, checked her watch. "Cleanup time," she announced. "You have ten minutes until the final bell."

"Hooray!" Bethany cried. "I can't wait!"

She turned to Natalie and confided, "After school, I'm going to ride my horse until dark."

"Wow," Natalie said. She ran her hands through her short dark hair. "I'd be scared to get on a horse."

"You wouldn't be if you went riding with me," Bethany said. She loved every kind of animal — from hamsters to rabbits to cows.

"The horse I ride is gentle," she added. "Her name is Shining Star."

"Are you talking about me?" Brianna interrupted. She put her hand on her hip. As usual, she was wearing the latest fashion. Today it was a pink miniskirt and a silver tank top. "*I'm* a shining star."

Once Bethany and Brianna had been best friends. Once Bethany had been Brianna's biggest fan. Once Bethany had cried "Yay, Brianna!" and "You're the best!" whenever Brianna bragged. But Bethany had finally gotten tired of being Brianna's personal cheerleader.

Now Bethany barely spoke to Brianna.

"I have a play rehearsal after school, then private conversation in French," Brianna announced.

"Really?" Bethany said. She took her notebook out of her desk and then turned toward Natalie. "Do you want to come with me tonight?" she asked Natalie. "I *know* you'd love Shining Star."

"I can't," Natalie said. "I'm going shopping with my mother. I'm getting new sneakers." She pointed to her old ones. They were white and splattered with paint. Her little toe was poking through one; the other was frayed and ripped.

"Another pair like those?" Bethany asked.

"Sure," Natalie said.

Brianna glanced at her shiny laced boots. "You ought to go to Superb Shoes. That's where the *best* shoes and boots are."

"We're going to the Sneaker Discount Warehouse," Natalie said.

"That's where I got these." Abby wiggled her toes in her purple sneakers.

"Those are so cute!" Bethany squealed.

"Those are so cute!" Mason mimicked.

Abby tried to think of a good comeback, but just then the final bell rang.

"School's over!" Natalie and Bethany cried, high-fiving each other.

Abby searched under the mess of papers in her desk for the books she needed to bring home. "I have to do homework after school and then do more homework after dinner," she complained to Mason.

"Wait until spring break," Mason said. "No homework for a week!"

"Get your coats, and leave the classroom in an orderly fashion," Ms. Kantor said.

The fifth-graders rushed toward the cloakroom.

Abby got her coat and headed for the door.

Once she would have waited for Jessica and Natalie and walked home with the two of them. Now Jessica was gone and Natalie and Bethany had become good friends. They spent more time with each other than with Abby.

Sometimes Abby went biking or Rollerblading with Casey, who was in the other fifth-grade class. Casey was a boy, but he was *not* Abby's boyfriend. She still did things with Natalie and Bethany — though not as often as before Jessica left.

It was good to have friends, but Abby missed having a best friend.

As Abby opened the front door of her house, her younger brother ran toward her. "Abby!" Alex yelled. "You got a letter!"

"From Jessica?" Abby said hopefully.

He shook his head no and waved the envelope at her. It was shiny and purple. There were pictures of boots and shoelaces decorating the front and back.

Abby recognized its sender immediately. "Grandma Emma!" she cried.

Grandma Emma was Abby's favorite relative. She sent letters in envelopes handmade from magazine pages. She collected salt and pepper shakers shaped like animals, people, and famous buildings. She sent Abby calendars for her birthday.

Abby's calendar collection was famous in the fifth grade. She had old ones, new ones, animal, plant, and mineral ones. She had historic calendars, funny calendars, art calendars, scenic calendars, musical calendars. . . .

"Open the letter," Alex commanded.

"Your shirt is buttoned wrong," Abby said.

"So?" Alex often wore mismatched socks and inside-out shirts. Once he even wore pajamas to school. It didn't bother him in the least.

Abby carefully opened the envelope and took out a sheet of rainbow-colored paper.

"Read it out loud," Alex urged. He peered over her shoulder.

Abby snatched the letter away.

"Nosy!" she scolded. "It's for me, not you."

Alex pretended to sulk.

"All right," Abby said. "I'll read it out loud."

"Dear Abby,

"As I write this letter, I am sitting on a park bench and Zipper is chasing squirrels up trees. It's a warm, sunny day, and there are crocuses along the path. This afternoon I'm going to rake my garden.

"Would you like to visit me over spring break?"

Abby stopped reading. *"Yes!"* she yelled, pumping her fist in the air. "Grandma Emma saves the day! I mean, the week," she added.

"No fair!" Alex cried, but he was smiling, too.

"It's *my* turn to be with Grandma Emma," Abby reminded him. Last year, Abby's sister Eva had flown out to spend time with Grandma Emma alone. The year before, it was her other sister, Isabel. Eva and Isabel were fourteen-year-old twins.

"When you're old enough, *you'll* get to go, too," Abby said to her brother. She began to read the letter again.

"Your cousin Cleo will be staying with me, too. Her

parents are flying to London for a week. She is going to attend an arts program here in the city. Would you like to join her? Since you're both ten years old and in fifth grade, you'll have a lot in common. We'll celebrate your birthday at the end of the week.

"Lots of love,

"Grandma Emma

"P. S. Zipper is barking. I think he's trying to send a message, too. Come see us soon!"

Chapter 2

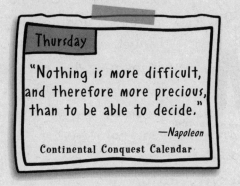

Thursday

"Nothing is more difficult, and therefore more precious, than to be able to decide."

—Napoleon

Continental Conquest Calendar

It's not difficult for _me_ to decide what to do!

I want to attend an arts program and visit Grandma Emma! I want to celebrate my birthday with her!

Even if cousin Cleo is also there.

I wish I didn't have to share Grandma Emma! I want her all to myself! But it's better to share Grandma Emma than not to see her at all.

I have made my decision! It was easy.

My parents haven't made theirs. They're worried that I'm too young to fly alone.

Isabel and Eva flew on their own. <u>Why not me???</u>

Because, according to Mom and Dad, my sisters were twelve and thirteen, not ten.

<u>SO??????</u>

I'm a very mature ten! And I'll be a year older at the end of spring break.

Mom and Dad <u>have</u> to let me get on the plane by myself!

Otherwise I won't get to see Grandma Emma!

Otherwise I'll have to spend spring break — and my birthday — at home, without a best friend!

Ms. Bunder shook a shoe box full of papers. "Today's creative writing exercise is called Word Jumble," she announced with a smile.

Only a few years ago, Ms. Bunder was baby-sitting Ms. Kantor's kids. Now she was teaching creative writing to Ms. Kantor's class.

She didn't look much older than Isabel or Eva. Today she wore a pale blue skirt and a matching shirt. Her earrings were silver.

"You're each going to take a word or two from this box," Ms. Bunder announced, "and then write a story or a poem about it."

"Yay!" Abby cheered. Creative writing was her favorite subject, and Ms. Bunder was her favorite teacher.

"Word Jumble?" Brianna repeated with a curl of her lip. "It sounds like a garage sale."

"The words *garage sale* are in the box," Ms. Bunder said. "Maybe you'll pick them, Brianna."

"I never buy anything at garage sales, Ms. Bunder!" Brianna protested with a toss of her head. "All *my* clothes are new."

"Garage sales are the best!" Mason cried. "Last week I found a skateboard for four dollars!"

"I love garage sales!" Abby agreed. She had held one in her yard and had earned enough money to buy new Rollerblades.

"Brianna hates garage sales; Mason and Abby like them," Ms. Bunder said. "If all three of them wrote about this topic, they'd each have something unique to say about it."

Ms. Bunder continued. "Pick a word or phrase

from the box, and see what it brings up for you. Memories or thoughts? Feelings or ideas? Then write your story or poem."

"Could we write both?" Abby asked. "A story *and* a poem?"

"If you have time," Ms. Bunder said. She walked between the desks, allowing each student to pick out one slip of paper from the shoe box. "Don't peek! Be surprised!"

Natalie plucked a paper from the box. *"Magic,"* she read. She was wearing new, unstained white sneakers. "That's one of my favorite words."

"The more a word suggests to you, the better," Ms. Bunder said.

"I hope I get *hamster*," Bethany said. "Then I can write about Blondie." Blondie was Bethany's beloved pet hamster.

Brianna sniffed. "Is that all you think about?"

Bethany didn't answer. She took a word from the box, glanced at it, and sat thinking.

Mason was next. He burped, grabbed, and chuckled. "Got a good one!"

"Your turn, Abby." Ms. Bunder held out the shoe box.

Abby closed her eyes and let her fingers sink to the bottom. She pulled out a slip of paper and unfolded it on her desk. *"Travel,"* it said.

Travel. She hoped it was in her future. Or maybe it was her fortune.

"Ms. Bunder, this is like a fortune cookie," Abby said.

"Fortunes?" Ms. Bunder repeated. "Great idea, Abby. Why don't you write some?"

Abby's eyes lit up. She grabbed a sheet of paper and her purple pen.

This is what I like about Ms. Bunder. I have a little bit of an idea, and she makes it bigger.

Writing fortunes will be <u>funnnnnnnnnnn</u>!!!!!!!

I love creative writing!

I love being in Ms. Bunder's class!

She never says, "That's not a good idea!" or "Quiet! Do the assignment!"

She never gets mad at anyone for saying what he or she thinks.

She always makes our ideas and thoughts sound really exciting!

If Ms. Bunder taught creative writing all day long, I'd _never_ want school to end!!!!

Abby doodled in the margins of her paper. Suddenly the ideas began to flow.

<u>Travel Cookies</u>

Eat the whole bag and have all your fortunes come true!

Fortune #1. You will travel very far during spring vacation.

Fortune #2. You will take a long journey by airplane.

Fortune #3. Great things come to those who travel.

Fortune #4. Travel is in your future!

Fortune #5. Travel will reunite old friends and relatives.

Fortune #6. Long trips are lucky.

Fortune #7. A mysterious cousin will change your life.

Fortune #8. The unknown beckons.

Fortune #9. Parents cooperate to send you far away.

Fortune #10. Those who travel light, travel with a light heart.

Ms. Bunder glanced at the clock. "We'll share our writing in just a minute," she announced.

Abby frowned and began to write more quickly.

Fortune #11. Mile by mile, travel with a smile.

Fortune #12. Travel brings surprises.

"Time's up!" Ms. Bunder said. "Who wants to read first?"

Brianna stood up. "Me first." She flounced to the front of the room. "My word was *twilight* — or as they say in Paris, *l'heure bleue.*"

"The whatty-what?" Natalie asked.

"The blue hour," Brianna explained with an airy wave of her hand. "In French, it means twilight."

Bethany rolled her eyes.

"Twilight," Brianna continued, "is the time when my French tutor tells me that I have the best accent he's ever heard. At twilight, I'm often onstage, re-hearsing my part in the play. I've got a leading role, and I'm the only young person in the cast. It's re-markable, the director says."

"That's not about twilight," Natalie murmured. "It's about Brianna."

"Everything is," Abby whispered back.

Brianna finished reading her essay. It was five pages long.

"Was that a creative writing story?" Bethany whis-pered.

"It was an advertisement," Abby replied.

"Or a paid political announcement," Natalie said.

"For president of the Briannacan party," Abby murmured. "Brianna can speak French, Brianna can star in plays, Brianna can do everything best — "

"Sshh!" Bethany nudged her and pointed to the front of the room. Zach had started to read.

He had taken the word *vacation* and written a poem about computers.

Tyler had used the words *mushroom soup* to write a story about computers.

Jonathan had picked *frantic*. He had written a story about computers, too.

Mason broke the mold. He used the word *ah-choo*

to write a story about a sneeze that destroyed the world.

Finally it was Abby's turn. She read her travel fortunes.

"I wish I had written fortunes, too!" Bethany cried. "What about: 'You will realize your dream of becoming a veterinarian'? My word is *dream*."

"You will dream of hamsters every night for a month," Abby joked.

Ms. Bunder waved her hand to get everyone's attention.

"I have an idea!" she announced. "We'll write fortunes for our next creative writing assignment! When we're done, we'll mix them all up, and each of us will pick one."

"What if they really happen?" Natalie asked.

"That'll be our *next* creative writing project! We'll write about how our fortune does or doesn't come true," Ms. Bunder said.

The fifth-graders applauded. Another fun assignment from Ms. Bunder.

Ms. Bunder can make a creative writing exercise out of anything, Abby thought. She looked down at her page again. She wondered if any of her fortunes would come true. She hoped they would.

Chapter 3

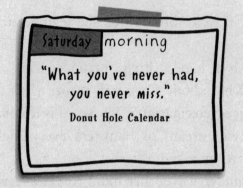

Saturday morning

"What you've never had,
you never miss."

Donut Hole Calendar

<u>Oh, yeah?</u>

I've never spent spring break
with Grandma Emma, but if my
parents don't let me go, I'll
miss it!

I'll miss flying alone on a
plane for the first time.

I'll miss the arts program
Grandma Emma wants to enroll me in.

I'll miss celebrating my birthday with
Grandma Emma.

(I probably won't miss spending time with my cousin Cleo.)

Abby skipped down the stairs and ran into the kitchen. She smelled coffee and French toast. Dirty dishes were stacked in the sink.

Her father was unloading the dishwasher. "Give me a hand, will you, Abby?" He held out a stack of plates.

"But I—" Abby started to protest but then stopped. She was going to be on her best behavior so her parents would let her travel by herself to Grandma Emma's.

She opened the cupboard and placed the clean dishes on a shelf.

"Yes, yes," her mother said, tapping her fingers against the kitchen table. Olivia Hayes was talking on the phone.

As usual on a Saturday morning, Abby's mother was wearing sweatpants, an old T-shirt, and sneakers.

On weekdays, Olivia Hayes worked long hours as a lawyer. On weekends, she jogged and gardened and spent time with the family. She went to games and plays and rehearsals.

Abby thought it was like having two different mothers.

Paul Hayes worked at home as a freelance Web page designer. The Hayes children usually saw more of their father than their mother.

"Who's she talking to, Dad?" Abby whispered.

"The airlines," Paul Hayes said.

"For *me*?" Abby almost shouted.

Her father put his finger to his lips. "Be patient," he said. "We're checking into fares and policies on unaccompanied minors."

"Minors," Abby repeated. "It sounds like baseball."

Her father smiled. "Minor means you. A ten-year-old traveling by herself. We're not sure — "

He was interrupted by Olivia Hayes. "Can you hand me the credit card?" she said. "I need to give the number to the agent."

"Credit card?" Abby said.

Her father reached for his wallet. He riffled through the cards and pulled one out, then handed it to Abby's mother.

"Am I going?" Abby asked eagerly. "Are you making a reservation?"

Her mother acted as if she hadn't heard Abby's question. She began to read out the credit card number.

"Patience," her father said again.

Abby groaned.

"Okay, that's for next week," her mother said. "A direct flight so she won't have to transfer. She's ten years old. She'll be met by her grandmother at the airport."

"I *am* going!" Abby shouted. She jumped up. "Hooray!"

Olivia Hayes turned to Abby and put her finger to her lips. "Sorry?" she said into the phone. "I didn't catch that. All right. Thank you."

She hung up the phone and glanced at her husband. "Good news," she said. "Ten years old is not too young to fly alone."

"That's great," Paul Hayes said.

"Does this mean — ?" Abby said.

Her mother smiled at her. "Start packing your bags," she said. "You're going to Grandma Emma's."

"Your move," Abby said to Bethany.

Bethany picked up the dice and shook them.

The three girls sat on the floor of Bethany's room. They had a board game in front of them and bags of pretzels and popcorn beside them.

Bethany's room was decorated with pictures of horses, cows, hamsters, ducks, and a poster of Bethany on a balance beam.

In her deluxe hamster cage, Blondie slumbered in a pile of shredded wood.

"I rolled a twelve!" Bethany cried. She moved ahead on the board. "I'm catching up with you, Nat-alie!"

"No one catches up with *me*," Natalie said, picking up the dice. "Eleven! I'm almost home!"

Abby picked up the dice and tossed them from one hand to another. "What are you doing for spring break?" she asked her friends.

A few hours earlier, Abby had called Grandma Emma to tell her the news. Her grandmother had been thrilled.

Abby hoped her friends would be happy for her, too. She hadn't told Bethany and Natalie yet — she wasn't sure why.

Bethany glanced at Natalie. "Natalie and I are taking riding lessons over spring break," she announced.

"You are?" Abby said in amazement to Natalie. "I thought you were afraid of horses."

"Bethany and I went riding together two nights ago. It was great."

"Wow," Abby stammered. She felt left out. Why hadn't they invited her?

She rolled the dice and advanced three spaces. Bethany was gaining on Natalie, but Natalie threw another twelve.

"I'm the winner!" Natalie cried. "Another game, anyone?"

"No!" Bethany said. "You win *all* the time!" She passed an open bag of pretzels to Abby. "Have some."

Abby shook her head. "No, thanks."

"Isn't your birthday soon?" Bethany asked. "It's during the break, isn't it? Are you having a party?"

"I'm not having a party this year," Abby said. "I won't be here."

"But I already found the perfect present for you!" Bethany protested.

"Save it for next year," Abby said. "It's a calendar, I hope. I won't mind if it's a year old."

" 'There was a fifth-grader who lived in a shoe,' " Natalie sang. " 'She had so many calendars, she didn't know what to do.' "

"Is that the way the nursery rhyme goes?" Bethany teased Natalie.

"Uh, duh," Natalie joked, holding out the bag of pretzels to her.

"I wish I had so many horses I didn't know what to do," Bethany said. "Or hamsters," she added, with a fond look at her sleeping pet.

"So where are you going?" Natalie asked Abby.

Abby took a breath. "I'm visiting my Grandma Emma. My cousin Cleo will be there, too," she said. "Our grandmother enrolled us both in an arts program for spring break."

"Nice," Bethany said.

"Uh-huh," Natalie agreed. "What's your cousin like?"

"I don't know," Abby said. "I haven't seen her since I was two. She dumped a bucket of sand on my head."

Her friends laughed.

"Her parents are professors. They travel all over the world," Abby continued. "France, Spain, India, Morocco, Russia . . . my family never sees them. My grandmother writes me letters about all the things Cleo does," Abby added. "She acts, she plays the piano, she speaks three languages, she swims — "

"She sounds like Brianna," Natalie interrupted.

"Oh, no!" Abby cried. "That's all I need — spring vacation with a Brianna clone."

What if Cleo was one of those girls who did every-thing perfectly? What if she got all of Grandma Emma's attention? *What if Grandma Emma liked Cleo better than she liked Abby?*

Abby put her head on her knees. Suddenly she didn't feel as excited about the trip as she had a few minutes ago.

She wished that Jessica were here: the old Jessica, not the new Jessy.

The old Jessica would have reassured Abby about her trip. She would have made Abby feel better about Cleo.

Abby shut her eyes and tried to hear Jessica's voice.

"Cleo's probably improved with age," Jessica would say.

At least she wouldn't be dumping buckets of sand on Abby's head.

"*No one* can brag as much as Brianna!" Jessica would add.

If Cleo was a bigger bragger than Brianna, Abby would give her a special page in the *Hayes Book of World Records*.

Abby glanced at Natalie and Bethany. They weren't trying to cheer her up or make her see the funny side of the situation. They were talking about horses.

They were still her friends, but . . . it wasn't the same now that Jessica was gone. Abby sometimes felt lonely even when she was with them.

It was good she was going away. Abby just hoped that Cleo wouldn't be worse than Brianna.

Chapter 4

Friday night

"A good traveler is one who does not know where he is going to, and a perfect traveler does not know where he came from."
—Lin Yutang

Hot Air Balloon Calendar

Where I'm going to: Grandma Emma's.
Where I came from: my house.

Does knowing where I'm going to and
   where I came from mean I'm a bad
   traveler? I hope not!!!
      Good travelers know how to
   pack.
      I packed my bags very care-
   fully. Everything fit into a small
   wheeled suitcase and a knapsack.

Abby's travel list

jeans and cargo pants
T-shirts and sweaters
pajamas with purple hearts
socks, striped and solid
purple tie-dyed underwear
rain jacket
sneakers
toothbrush and toothpaste
hairbrush and scrunchies
earrings (just in case Grandma Emma
    takes me to get my ears pierced)
journal and purple pen
book
apple, sandwich, and candy bar for the
    airplane
money

GUESS WHERE I'M WRITING THIS???

If you know the answer, you win a free
bag of airplane pretzels and a glass of
juice.
(That's all they give you to eat!! Good
thing I packed some food.)

The airplane is crowded. There is a man typing on a laptop next to me. Across the aisle, a woman is sleeping.

We're flying above the clouds. They look like giant pillows. I wish I could somer-sault from one to another. Or have a pillow-cloud fight with Natalie and Bethany.

<u>Only ten more minutes and we'll be there!!!</u>

Later Friday night

Grandma Emma was waiting for me when I came out of the plane. So was Cleo.

<u>Cousin Cleo - a description</u>

1. She has short light-brown hair.
2. She wears big glasses on her skinny face.
3. Her elbows are bony.
4. Her fingernails are short and polished dark blue.
5. She is wearing a short pink skirt and a halter top.
6. <u>Her ears are pierced!</u>

Cousin Cleo — a conversation

Abby (friendly): Wow, I can't believe you have pierced ears! You're so lucky! Your parents let you?

Cleo frowns and doesn't say anything.

Abby (repeats): I mean, uh, your parents? They let you get your ears pierced?

Cleo still doesn't reply.

Abby: Oh, uh . . . never mind.

Cleo (quietly): I got it done while they were away.

Abby: What did they say?

Cleo: Nothing. They didn't notice.

Abby: <u>Lucky!</u>

Cleo (snaps): Your parents probably notice <u>everything</u> you do!

Cousin Cleo — a conclusion

She's a pill! (I wish someone — besides Grandma Emma — would take her!)

The best thing about Cleo (so far):

The worst thing about Cleo (so far):
Grandma Emma thinks she's the best.
(Why? Why? <u>Why?</u>)

<u>Conversation in car</u>:
Grandma Emma: My two favorite ten-year-old granddaughters together at last!
Grandma Emma: You'll finally get to know each other!

Grandma Emma: Zipper is excited, too. He wanted to come with me to the airport, but I had to leave him at home.
Grandma Emma: Wait until you start the arts program! You'll both love it!
Grandma Emma: And I know you're going to love each other.
Grandma Emma: You have so much in common.

<u>What Cleo said</u>:

<u>What Abby said</u>:

<u>What happened next after the exciting</u>
<u>three-way conversation</u>:

1. Grandma Emma pulled into her garage.
2. She turned off the ignition and said, "We're home at last!"
3. Inside the house, Zipper started barking like crazy.
4. Grandma Emma unlocked the door to her house. Zipper, a small, black, excitable dog, bounded out and jumped on Cleo and me.
5. Cleo said, "Snookums, Widdy Zippy!!!" (Boy, is she weird!!)
6. I said, "Good dog, Zipper." (Cleo looked at me like I was weird!!!)
7. Grandma Emma called us in to help with dinner. She had Cleo wash the lettuce for a salad. She had me set the table.
8. We ate dinner. Grandma Emma talked the whole time.

P.S. Grandma Emma's house is filled with salt and pepper sets. She has salt and pepper shakers in the shapes of buildings, cats, mermaids, cows, mushrooms, rockets, birds, the Empire State Building, aliens, and shoes. Her salt and pepper shaker collection is almost as good as my calendar collection!!!

After dinner, we called our families to let them know that we had arrived safely. No one was home at my house so I had to leave a message. (Boo-hoo!)

Cleo calls her parents "Alicia" and "Robert." She speaks to them in French and Spanish.

The Great Bag Unpack
by Abby Hayes

And now, ladies and gentlemen, we bring you the two ten-year-old cousin contestants, Abby Hayes and Cleo Wayne!!!

On the left side of the guest bedroom is Cousin Cleo.

She gets the bed with the silly pink ruffles. (Ha, ha, ha.) Her bed has a bookcase for a headboard. (Boo-hoo, I want one, too!)

On the right side is Abby.
She gets the bed with the
purple flowers. (Ha-ha-ha.)
Her bed has a reading lamp
attached to the headboard.
(Ha-ha-ha again.) She can
read in bed – or write in her
journal!

Cleo is unpacking a large,
beat-up green suitcase. It has stickers all
over its front and back. It looks like it's
traveled everywhere in the world.

Abby is unpacking a small, new, wheeled
suitcase that has no stickers. It has only
made one trip.

Which cousin will empty her bag faster???
Which cousin will put away her clothes
first?
Which one will Grandma Emma praise?
(Grandma Emma says that the winner gets
to choose a movie to watch before bed!)

Ladies and gentlemen, Cleo is tossing

clothes all over her bed! They are mostly fashionable skirts and tops in pink, yellow, and turquoise. She has also brought a lap-top computer!

And a small jewelry case that looks as if it might hold earrings!

Abby is neatly folding jeans and cargo pants, striped shirts and socks, purple underwear and pajamas, and putting them away in drawers.

Neither contestant speaks to the other.

After a while, Grandma Emma knocks at the door. "Do we have a winner yet?"

Abby's things are almost all folded and put away, while Cleo's are still spread out all over the bed.

Suddenly Cleo grabs everything and shoves it into a drawer.

"Done!" she yells, kicking the drawer shut with her foot.

Before Abby can even say "No fair," Grandma Emma enters the room and declares Cleo the winner.

Chapter 5

Saturday | <u>very</u> early morning

"There's nothing new under the sun."

Novelty Calendar

(There's <u>everything</u> new under the sun!)

And there's lots new under Grandma Emma's roof:
1. Me
2. Cleo
3. Cleo's pajamas
   (They are bright yellow, decorated with a picture of pancakes.)

<u>Pancakes??????</u>

Cleo talks in her sleep. She thrashes around and hits the pillow. Once she woke up and turned on the light. She got out her laptop and wrote for a few minutes before going back to bed.

I asked her what she was writing. She said it was an idea.

(There's only one good idea in the middle of the night: SLEEP!)

The strange noises in Grandma Emma's house also kept waking me up. Like Zipper barking. The pipes banging. The floorboards creaking.

The room we're in has gold-and-blue wallpaper. It has one small window.

I miss my purple room! I miss my calendars! I miss Alex and Eva and Isabel!!! (Well . . . maybe . . . a little bit.) I miss my cat, T-Jeff. I hope Isabel is petting him twice as much as usual.

I miss Mom and Dad!!!

The only fun thing I brought from home was my journal. Thank goodness for my —

CLEO ALERT!! She is getting up. I'm going to stop writing now!

"Good morning!" Grandma Emma was flipping pancakes at the stove. "Did you sleep well? Was the bed comfortable? Are you hungry?"

"Sure," Abby said to all of her grandmother's questions. She ran her fingers through her damp, just-washed hair. It was already curling wildly.

"Sit down," her grandmother told her. "Pancakes hot off the grill. First come, first served. Is Cleo up yet?"

"She just woke up." Abby sat down at the table. "She's taking a shower."

Abby had beat Cleo to the bathroom. Years of practice with Eva and Isabel had made her a champion of the Fifty-foot Bathroom Dash.

Cleo had straightened her glasses and snapped, "You better not use up all the hot water!"

Abby hoped Cleo's shower was cold and refreshing.

Grandma Emma brought over a stack of pancakes. "There's maple syrup," she said, pointing to a tin in the shape of a log cabin. "Or do you want jam?"

"Syrup, please," Abby said. She unscrewed the cap and drenched her pancakes.

Her grandmother went back to the griddle and

poured fresh batter on the hot pan. "So how are you and Cleo getting along?" she asked.

"Mmmm," Abby mumbled, pointing to her mouth full of pancakes.

"Isn't she wonderful?!" her grandmother continued. "I knew you'd love her! So talented! So intelligent! Such a terrific person! I'm so glad you're visiting me together!"

"Oh, yeah," Abby said, swallowing hard.

Cleo came into the kitchen. Her hair was wet and plastered to her head. She was wearing a short blue skirt and a white tank top. She had bracelets on her skinny arms and tiny flower earrings in her ears.

"Good morning," Cleo said to no one in particular.

"Did you have a good night's sleep?" Grandma Emma asked. "A nice hot shower? Ready for pancakes?"

"You always make my favorites!" Cleo said to Grandma Emma.

"Me, too," Abby said, after a moment.

Cleo picked up her plate and brought it over to the stove. "Thanks for making pancakes," she said as her grandmother piled them onto her plate.

"Thanks," Abby echoed.

She wished she had thought of saying it first.

Cleo took a seat across from Abby. The two girls didn't look at each other.

"Would you please pass the syrup?" Cleo said.

It wasn't fair! Abby thought. *Her cousin had grown-up manners* and *pierced ears.* Their grandmother turned off the flame under the griddle and wiped her hands on a towel. "Have a good breakfast, girls. We're headed out for a street fair and carnival downtown today."

"That sounds wonderful, Grammy," Cleo said.

"Yeah, great," Abby said. It would have been the perfect day — if Cleo wasn't there.

Grandma Emma, Cleo, and Abby threaded their way through narrow, crowded streets.

Clowns tumbled and mimes acted out stories. Music blared, vendors called out their wares, and small children shrieked with excitement.

Abby and Cleo had their faces painted. Abby had herself turned into a purple clown. Cleo had a small, delicate butterfly on her forehead. They saw a short play and watched a juggler eat fire.

As Abby stopped to look at a glassblowing exhibit,

a man jostled her. She stumbled off the sidewalk and into the street.

"Hey!" Abby protested. She steadied herself.

Grandma Emma rushed over. "Are you all right, honey?"

"I'm okay," Abby said. She wiggled her foot. "I almost twisted my ankle, though."

"We have to stay close to one another," Grandma Emma said, looking at the two girls. "Especially in these crowds."

"I'm fine," Abby repeated.

"Do you still have your money?" Cleo asked.

Abby put her hand in her pocket and pulled out a wrinkled ten-dollar bill. "Yes! See?"

"You're lucky," Cleo said. "You could have lost it all."

Abby frowned.

"Pickpockets push you, then steal your money," Cleo lectured. "That's how they do it. Didn't you know that?"

"Of course I knew that!" Abby lied.

"My mother had a hundred seventy-five dollars stolen in Europe — " Cleo stopped suddenly.

"Look!" she cried. "A magician!" She pointed at a

man in black jeans and a black T-shirt pulling scarves from a large hat. "I *love* magic!"

"Let's go see him!" Grandma Emma said.

Abby kept her hand in the pocket with her money. She wasn't going to lose it! Did her cousin think she was some sort of idiot?

The magician rode on a unicycle, pulling doves out of his hat. He stopped and asked for volunteers from the audience. Cleo raised her hand.

The magician picked someone else.

Good, Abby thought. *That'll show her.* She wondered how she was going to stand an entire week of Cleo Wayne.

Chapter 6

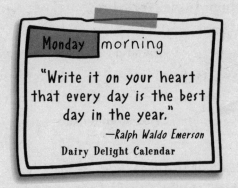

Monday morning

"Write it on your heart
that every day is the best
day in the year."
—*Ralph Waldo Emerson*
Dairy Delight Calendar

Yesterday wasn't. Grandma Emma sent
Cleo and me to the park so she could take
a nap.

Abby and Cleo's afternoon at the park:
Minutes spent walking: 35
Minutes spent getting snacks: 9
Minutes spent eating snacks: 13
Minutes spent wondering what else to do:
   41
Minutes spent talking to each other: 0

More memorable moments with Cleo:

1. Setting table for dinner: The War of the Forks

2. Tossing salad: All over the floor

3. Playing cards: Who cheated?

4. Choosing video: My turn!!

Worst moment in worst day:

Last night before bed, Cleo pulled out her laptop. "I'm writing a novel," she announced.

That's why she jots down ideas in the middle of the night.

If Cleo went to my school, my favorite teacher, Ms. Bunder, would probably <u>love</u> her. She'd think Cleo was a better writer than me. I'd have to listen to Ms. Bunder praise Cleo all the time — just the way Grandma Emma does!

Maybe <u>today</u> will be the best day in the year?

Today I helped Grandma Emma wash the breakfast

dishes. (I beat Cleo to it while she was brushing her teeth.)

Today is the first day of the arts program. Today I will get to be with a lot of kids who <u>aren't</u> Cleo.

<u>Cousin contest results</u>:
1. Abby has won the Fifty-foot Bathroom Dash for the past three days.
2. Cleo has won in the Grandmother Compliment category.
3. The two cousins have tied in the Fewest Words Spoken contest.

"These are my granddaughters, Cleo Wayne and Abby Hayes," Grandma Emma said to the woman in the front office of the Arts Center. "I've enrolled them for the spring break program."

The woman glanced at a sheet and checked off their names.

"Welcome," she said. "I know you'll enjoy the arts program. The day starts in our dance room. Go upstairs and turn left."

"Dance?" Abby said with a frown. "Are we dancing?" She thought an arts program meant drawing, painting, writing, and singing — not dancing. Dancing was the last thing she wanted to do.

"I love to dance!" Cleo said, striking a ballet pose.

"You're a terrific dancer," Grandma Emma said, with a smile. "I'm sure you are, too, Abby," she added.

"Not really," Abby muttered.

Grandma Emma kissed them both on the cheek. "I'm off!" she said. "Unless you want me to come upstairs with you."

"No, thanks!" Abby said.

"We're okay," Cleo seconded.

With a wave of her hand, Grandma Emma disappeared.

Without speaking, Abby and Cleo climbed the stairs to the dance room.

A group of more than two dozen girls and boys sat in a circle on the floor. As Abby and Cleo entered, many of them looked up.

Abby felt her cheeks get hot. She wondered if people were gaping at her red hair or her purple socks or her striped T-shirt.

Cleo wore her usual outfit of short skirt and tank top, with matching coral earrings. She was almost cute — except for the oversized glasses and her long, skinny arms.

Abby slid to the floor and sat in the first open place. She wanted to join the group. She didn't want to be noticed.

Cleo marched three times around the room. Finally she sat at the opposite end of the circle from Abby.

A man in khaki pants and a polo shirt hurried into the room.

"My name is Bill," he said. "Welcome to our arts program. There are two sections. One will be a theater and dance workshop. The other will be a picture bookmaking workshop. Your parents have already signed you up for one or the other — although it's still possible to change."

"We're writing books?!" Abby cried. This was even better than what she had imagined. Surely Grandma Emma would've signed her up for bookmaking — and, with any luck, signed Cleo up for theater and dance.

Abby noticed a girl with dark eyes and long black

braids. She had a serious expression on her face. When she saw Abby looking at her, she smiled.

She seems really nice, Abby thought. *I hope I get to know her.*

Bill unfolded a piece of paper. "Let's get started!" He began to read the names of those who were doing bookmaking and those who were in the theater group.

"Abby Hayes, bookmaking," Bill read. "Cleo Wayne, bookmaking!"

"I thought you loved theater and dancing," Abby called to Cleo.

Cleo adjusted her glasses. "I want to work on my writing," she said.

"Oh," Abby said.

Bill finished reading the lists. "Is everyone happy?" he called. "Anyone want to change groups? Speak up now!"

Abby crossed her fingers. She hoped Cleo would change her mind at the last minute and decide she *had* to dance and act.

No one spoke. Oh, well. She and Cleo would just have to avoid each other. It would probably be easier here than at Grandma Emma's.

"Theater group, wait here." Bill motioned to Abby

and Cleo's group. "Bookmakers, come with me," he said. "I'm taking you to the greenhouse room."

"The greenhouse room," Abby repeated to herself. It sounded mysterious and lovely. She hoped it was.

Bill led them into a room with skylights and large windows. There were plants on the sills and long tables with stacks of writing and art supplies. "Here they are, Rebecca," he said to a woman watering the plants.

"Great!" Rebecca said. She put down the watering can. "Welcome to all the young writers and illustrators," she said.

She looked older than Ms. Bunder and younger than Ms. Kantor. Her hair was in a ponytail. She had glasses and wore no makeup.

Unlike any teacher Abby had ever known, she sat down on a table, her legs dangling over the edge. Her feet were bare.

"Have a seat," Rebecca said, gesturing toward the other tables. "On the chairs, on the floor, wherever."

Abby and Cleo sat at opposite ends of the room. The girl with the long dark braids sat at Abby's table. She was in the bookmaking group, too.

"Hi, I'm Mira," she whispered to Abby, with a shy smile.

Abby introduced herself, too.

Rebecca started to talk about the workshop. Everyone stared at her bare feet while she spoke.

"We're making picture books," Rebecca announced. "Writing them, illustrating them, binding them. On Friday, we'll have an author's tea and a reading for families and friends."

An excited murmur spread through the room.

Rebecca jumped down from the table and took a book from a box. "Here's a picture book that I wrote and illustrated myself."

The room instantly became still.

"You're a published author?" a boy asked.

Rebecca nodded. "I've published nine books. They're up here on the desk if you want to see them."

Abby caught her breath. A real author was leading the workshop!

She glanced across the room at Cleo. Cleo looked excited, too. For a moment, Abby wished they were friends.

"We're going to work in pairs," Rebecca said. "To avoid confusion and hurt feelings, I will randomly assign partners." She crisscrossed the room, picking kids to work together. "It's also a way to make new friends."

Abby kept her fingers crossed. She hoped Rebecca would put her with Mira.

Chapter 7

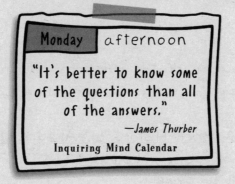

Monday afternoon

"It's better to know some
of the questions than all
of the answers."
—James Thurber

Inquiring Mind Calendar

Questions:

1. <u>Why</u> did Rebecca pair me with Cleo?
2. Why <u>did</u> Rebecca pair me with Cleo?
3. Why did Rebecca pair <u>me</u> with Cleo?
4. Why did Rebecca pair me with <u>Cleo</u>?

More questions:

1. Why?
2. WHY?
3. <u>WHY?</u>

<u>Answers</u>:

I know all of the questions and none of the answers. Is this better? Than <u>what</u>?

<u>A Brief History of Abby and</u>
<u>Cleo's Collaboration</u>
It will be brief.
Very, very, very brief.
Will it even happen?????

<u>A Play About a Workshop About a Book</u>
<u>About an Argument About . . .</u>
by Abby Hayes

Act I
A pleasant room with many windows, plants, sunlight, tables, pens, paper, and other assorted bookmaking supplies.

Rebecca, a published author, stands barefoot at the front of the room, talking to a group of kids.

Rebecca: The first rule of writing is, write what you know. Write from your own experience.

Boy: Like what?

Rebecca: Your own life, happy and sad events, your interests.

Boy: Outer space?

Rebecca: Why not?

Boy: I haven't been there.

Rebecca: But have you thought and dreamed and read about it?

Boy: Yes!

Rebecca: Then you know it. Thinking, dreaming, and reading count as experience, too.

Cleo: Can we write what we don't know?

Rebecca (laughs): There's an original idea! Try it and see!

Abby: What's the best kind of story to write?

Rebecca: A story that you want to write.

Mira: Do you have to like what you're writing about?

Rebecca: Not necessarily! You can write about things you love or hate.

Abby: How long does it take to write a picture book?

Rebecca: For me, anywhere from three months to three years. For you, a few days! Are you ready?

Chorus of Kids: <u>YES!!!!</u>

As the curtain falls, Cleo makes her way to the front of the room. She tells Rebecca that she's working on a novel. Rebecca looks impressed.

Abby is nervous. Is Cleo going to try to show her up?

Act II

The curtain rises again on the same scene. This time Abby and Cleo sit facing each other at a table. They are trying to collaborate on a book.

Abby: I have an idea about two best friends and one of them moves away.

Cleo: No! What about a ten-year-old girl who's a musical genius?

Abby: Too much like Brianna!

Cleo: Who's she?

Abby: A V.O.P.

Cleo: A <u>what</u>?

Abby: A Very Obnoxious Person.

Cleo: Oh.

Abby: What about a girl who sneaks a cat into her house without her family finding out?

Cleo: That could never happen!

Abby: Oh, yeah?

Cleo: I want to write about a thief who steals money at street fairs.

Abby: Ho-hum.

Cleo (challenging): Can you do better?

Abby: A swimming contest between boys and girls.

Cleo: Boring! How about a brother-sister war?

Abby: I'd rather write about a girl trying to make a soccer team.

Cleo: Soccer? Lacrosse is better!

The curtain rises and falls many times, always on the scene of Abby and Cleo arguing.

As they continue to argue, a narrator

steps to the front of the stage and addresses the audience.

Narrator: This is the first real conversation that Abby and Cleo have had. I don't think they'll ever agree. Will they get around to writing the book? _Nah!_

Abby (loudly): I'm not telling you any more of my ideas!
Cleo (loudly): I'm not telling you any more of mine, either!

As the curtain falls, the two cousins are still arguing.

THE PLAY ENDS
but the argument continues
and continues
and continues
and continues . . .

Enough already!

Rebecca just came over to our table.

Both Cleo and I asked to switch partners. (The first time we have agreed!)

"Everyone but you has already begun their stories," Rebecca pointed out. "I can't break up a working partnership. Cleo, with your writing talent, it should be easy. If you start, then Abby can help."

"But I'm good at writing, too!" I cried.

"And you couldn't find one single idea that you both liked?" Rebecca asked. "I find that hard to believe!"

"No," Cleo and I said in unison. (The second time we have agreed!)

Rebecca thought for a moment. "You'll just have to work separately for now," she said. "Both of you will have to write your own story. Tomorrow I'll help you choose one of the two to illustrate and bind into a book. Okay?"

"Yes," Cleo said, looking as if her story had already been chosen.

"Why can't we just work alone?" I said. "Each do her own book?"

Rebecca shook her head. "This workshop is about collaboration. Everyone else is working in pairs. If you don't want to do it, maybe you should switch to theater and dance."

"I want to do it," I said quickly.

"Me, too," Cleo said.

NOTE TO SELF: Will give self entire page in <u>Hayes Book of World Records</u> for Greatest Sacrifice for Art.

I love writing <u>so much</u> that I'll even work with Cleo!

I <u>might</u> even illustrate her story!

<u>Noooooooooo, that can't happen.</u> Rebecca HAS to choose <u>mine</u>!

P.S. Mira told me that she loves to illustrate. She would have been the *perfect* partner! Boo-hoo! Boo-hoo! <u>Boo-hoo!</u>

Chapter 8

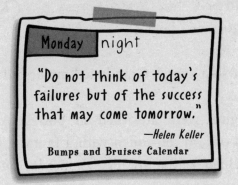

Monday night

"Do not think of today's failures but of the success that may come tomorrow."
—Helen Keller
Bumps and Bruises Calendar

<u>Don't think about</u>:
1. "Collaborating" with Cleo.
2. Rebecca possibly choosing Cleo's story.

<u>Think about</u>:
1. The story I'm writing (I have a great idea!).
2. Rebecca will love it!
3. She will realize that <u>I</u> am a talented writer, too!!!!
4. My story will be chosen over Cleo's.
5. The other kids will be amazed — especially Mira.

6. I will read my story at the author's tea and impress Grandma Emma!

"Look at you two," Grandma Emma said to Abby and Cleo.

Both girls were absorbed in books. Abby was stretched out on the couch with a fantasy; Cleo was in the recliner with a mystery. Zipper lay on the floor between them.

At dinner, Grandma Emma had asked them what they each liked best about the arts program.

Abby raved about Rebecca and bookmaking. Cleo told Grandma Emma about the author's tea on Friday.

Neither of them had told Grandma Emma that they had been assigned as writing partners in the workshop. Or that they couldn't agree on anything.

Grandma Emma peered out the window. "What a beautiful evening," she said. "We have to take a walk."

Abby and Cleo kept reading.

"Did either of you hear me?" Grandma Emma asked. "Let's make hay while the sun shines. Or before it sets," she joked.

Abby lifted her head from her book. "Casey would

have said, 'Let's make Hayes while the sun shines.' "

"Is she one of your friends?" her grandmother asked.

"He," Abby corrected. "He likes to make jokes out of my name. He's in the other fifth-grade class."

Cleo was staring curiously at her. "A *boy* is your friend?"

Abby ignored her cousin. She turned a page in her book.

"Get up! Shut those books! Now!" Grandma Emma softened her command with a smile.

"I'd love to take a walk, Grandma Emma," Cleo said.

"Me, too!" Abby cried. She grabbed a sweater. Cleo was already at the door, holding it open for Grandma Emma.

Grandma Emma picked up her house keys. She put Zipper on a leash. "Ready?"

"Ready," Abby said.

"Ready," Cleo echoed.

They scowled at each other.

"Which direction?" their grandmother asked.

"Left," Abby said.

"Right," Cleo said at exactly the same moment.

"Hmmm," their grandmother said.

"These are my granddaughters, Cleo and Abby." Grandma Emma proudly introduced them to a neighbor who was sweeping her front porch steps. "They're ten years old."

"Are you twins?" the neighbor asked Abby and Cleo. She was a short woman with dyed yellow hair.

"No!" they cried at the same time.

Abby glanced at Cleo. She didn't look anything like her, did she? Cleo had an equally horrified expression on her face.

"My two bookworms," Grandma Emma said fondly.

"Hello, Stuart," Grandma Emma said to a burly man digging up a patch of earth in front of his house. "More flower beds?"

"Roses," he grunted. He petted Zipper, then nodded to Cleo and Abby. "Your grandkids?"

Grandma Emma put an arm around each of them. "First cousins — getting to know each other."

"I thought they were sisters," the man said.

"Not sisters," Grandma Emma repeated. "They should be, though. They have so much in common."

Cleo and Abby glared at each other.

It was late. They had returned from the walk and had eaten a snack of cookies and milk. Zipper was in the backyard for the night. The curtains were drawn.

"Time to get ready for bed!" Grandma Emma said to Cleo and Abby, who were reading again. "You can read in bed for a little while," she promised.

Abby brushed her teeth and got into her pajamas. She climbed into bed with her book. She angled the lamp onto the open book and began to read again.

Across from her, Cleo held a flashlight over her mystery novel.

"Why don't you turn on the overhead light?" Abby suggested.

"I like reading with a flashlight," Cleo said.

"Isn't it uncomfortable?" Abby asked.

"No." Cleo moved the flashlight rapidly over the page.

Abby put down her book and picked up her journal.

<u>Cleo</u>

Adults love her.
I don't.

Adults think she's brilliant.

I think she's weird and obnoxious.
I do not like Cleo Wayne. I do not like Cleo Wayne. I do not like Cleo Wayne. I do not li –

"What are you writing?" Cleo asked.

Abby slammed her journal shut. "Nothing."

Cleo straightened her glasses on her nose. "I used to write in notebooks," she said. "But I haven't since Alicia and Robert gave me a laptop for my birthday. My novel is on it, and so is my journal."

"You keep a journal?" Abby couldn't help asking. She wondered if Cleo wrote in it every day.

"Of course," Cleo said. She focused her flashlight back on her book.

Abby didn't say anything. She opened her journal again.

Of course Cleo writes her journal on a laptop!

Of course she's writing a novel, too!

Of course she got a laptop for her birthday!

(And of course she has pierced ears!)

She is so much better than me at <u>every-thing!</u>

What am I going to get for <u>my</u> birthday?
1. An airplane ticket
   (already got it).
2. A calendar from
   Grandma Emma (her
   usual present).

3. A happy birthday greeting from Cleo
   (ONLY to impress Grandma Emma).
4. Clip-on earrings? (I'll probably get the
   sticker kind!)

Win a Fabulous Prize! Vote on the
World's Most Terrible Idea for the <u>Hayes
Book of World Records</u>:
   a) spending my birthday at home without
Jessica
   b) spending my birthday here with Cleo

The winner will receive a free copy of
<u>The Book That We Don't Want to Write
Together</u> by Abby Hayes and Cleo Wayne.

Chapter 9

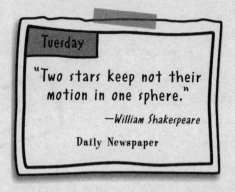

Tuesday

"Two stars keep not their motion in one sphere."

—William Shakespeare

Daily Newspaper

Grandma Emma read this quote in the paper today.

Grandma Emma: What do you think it means?

Abby: Stars are far apart so they don't collide or explode.

Cleo: They avoid each other.

Abby: They each live in their own universe.

Cleo: Stars are lucky. They don't have to spend time together if they don't want to.

Grandma Emma: I think the quote is about people.

Abby: It _is_?

Grandma Emma: It means that people act in different ways. They're not always on the same page. They sometimes can't cooperate with each other.

THAT'S FOR SURE!!!

Does Grandma Emma suspect that Cleo and I aren't getting along? We'll never keep our "motion in one sphere" – even if we have to share a room, an arts program, a bookmaking project, AND a favorite grandmother.

The sun came through the windows of the greenhouse room. As the kids worked on their stories, Rebecca moved from table to table, giving encouragement, advice, and suggestions.

At 11:02 A.M., Abby finished the last sentence of her story. She wrote "The End" with a huge flourish, stood up, and stretched.

At the other end of the table, Cleo scratched out some words. Her pad of paper was covered with scrawls and smears. She tore off a sheet, threw it on top of a pile of crumpled pages, and continued on a fresh page.

Rebecca came over to their table. "How are you doing? Need any help?"

"I'm done!" Abby announced.

Today Rebecca was wearing sandals with brightly colored socks, jeans, and a T-shirt. She told the group earlier that morning that her feet had gotten cold yesterday.

"Me, too!" Cleo cried, although she was still writing. She ripped off another sheet, threw down her pen, and gathered a pile of pages together.

"I finished first!" Abby said.

"Only by two minutes," Cleo insisted.

"So?" Abby said.

Rebecca shook her head. "What is it with you two?"

"Whose story are you going to read first?" Cleo asked.

"I'm going to read them *both* right now." Rebecca sat down at their table. "Go over to the art shelves, and check out the materials. Do you want to use watercolors, acrylic paint, pastels, cut paper, collage, colored pencils . . . ?"

"Colored pencils!" Abby said.

"Watercolors!" Cleo said.

Rebecca sighed. "I should have known. Why doesn't one of you draw and the other color? That way you can work together," she suggested. "I'll let you know when I'm done reading your stories."

Without speaking, Cleo and Abby headed toward the shelves.

Mira was arranging cutout pictures on a sheet of paper. As Abby and Cleo passed, she glanced up and smiled.

I wish she were my partner, Abby thought again.

"Are you doing a collage?" Abby asked her.

Mira nodded.

"I love collage!" Abby exclaimed. "But isn't it hard to illustrate a book that way?"

"Not really," Mira said. She had a soft, gentle voice.

"We could do that for our book," Abby said to Cleo. "Collage and drawings together."

"Paste makes the pages all crinkly," Cleo said.

Mira shook her head. "Not if you use poster-board."

Abby went over to the art supply shelf. "Look at this! Magazine photos, handmade papers, feathers! We could use it all!"

Cleo frowned. "It's not right for my story."

"You don't know which story Rebecca will choose," Abby warned her.

"Mine will be chosen," Cleo said confidently.

"Oh, *really*?" Abby said.

Mira looked at them curiously. "Aren't you working together as partners?"

Cleo and Abby glanced at each other, then looked quickly away.

"Well, yes," Cleo said. "I mean no."

"You see — " Abby began and then stopped. She didn't have a chance to explain because Rebecca was calling them.

"Very unusual," Rebecca said.

"Mine or hers?" Abby asked.

Rebecca didn't answer. The stories lay in front of her. She picked them both up and flipped through the pages. "This is *definitely* a first."

"Whose is a first?" Cleo asked.

"You mean — ?" Abby was confused. Did Rebecca like her story or Cleo's best?

"You'll have to see for yourselves," Rebecca said.

She passed Cleo's story to Abby and Abby's story to Cleo. "Read these now."

<u>Crazy Cousin</u>
by Cleo Wayne

Once upon a time, there lived two cousins. They lived together in a gingerbread house with their sweet old Grammy Mammy. The brown-haired cousin, an orphan whose name was Clover, tried hard to help her sweet old Grammy Mammy make ends meet. She worked hard to make everyone proud of her. She won prizes in writing, acting, and piano. All her grades were good. She had excellent manners.

The red-haired cousin, whose name was Agatha, had grown up in a loving family, but she took things for granted. She didn't care about manners or prizes. Her clothes were old and baggy. She didn't help dear old Grammy Mammy as much as she could. She ignored other people. All she thought about was herself.

Abby gasped.

Cleo was scowling as she read Abby's story.

Cousin Confusion
by Abby Hayes

There once lived two cousins of the same age who were as different as could be. The first cousin was sensitive, intelligent, kind, serious, and funny. Her eyes were blue, her hair was red. She loved to Rollerblade, pet her cat, and write stories. Her name was Alexandra.

The second cousin had beautiful clothes, pierced ears, and fancy computers, but she wasn't exactly friendly. Adults loved her, but kids didn't. She wore big glasses on her teeny-tiny face. Her name was Cuddy.

The two cousins were going to another country together to visit their kind, loving grandmother.

The two cousins faced each other.

"I do *not* have a teeny-tiny face!" Cleo said. "And lots of people love me, Alexandra!"

"*I* don't wear old, baggy clothes," Abby said. "And I help Grandma Emma a lot!"

Cleo's voice got more shrill. "Kids like me!"

"I do not ignore people!" Abby yelled. *"Clover!"*

It was suddenly quiet in the room. Writing and illustration stopped as everyone stared at the two cousins.

"Settle down, both of you!" Rebecca ordered. "This is fiction!" She looked from one to another. "Isn't it?"

Neither Cleo nor Abby said a word.

Rebecca put her hands on her hips. "Let's see," she began. "The two of you didn't want to collaborate. But you both wrote on the same subject, in a similar style, with similar characters who have opposite roles." She stopped. "Are you *really* cousins?"

Abby and Cleo nodded.

"Oh!" Rebecca cried. "Why didn't you tell me right away?"

Abby looked at Cleo. Cleo looked at Abby.

"I never thought of it," Abby said.

"Can't we change partners?" Cleo asked. *"Please?"*

"You know it's too late," Rebecca said. She looked over at the rest of the group. "It was too late yesterday, and now it's impossible."

Abby groaned.

"Go back to work!" Rebecca ordered everyone. She turned to Abby and Cleo. "The pen is mightier than the sword! Be careful how you use words."

"I know that quote," Abby muttered.

Rebecca shook her head. "What am I going to do with you two?"

"I *won't* illustrate her story!" Cleo said.

"Me, neither!" Abby said. "I mean, I won't illustrate *hers*, either!"

Chapter 10

Wednesday

"Nothing happens to anybody
which he is not fitted by
nature to bear."

—*Marcus Aurelius*

Powder Puff Calendar

Oh, yeah?

Things I can't bear:
1. Cleo.
2. Collaborating on a book with Cleo.
3. Having to illustrate Cleo's horrid, dis-
   gusting, revolting, nasty, stupid, pa-
   thetic, idiotic, ridiculous story.
4. Cleo illustrating my story! Or should I
   say <u>destroying</u> my story?
5. Reading "our" book together at the author's tea.

We pause for a moment of silent frustration.

Rebecca decided that the two stories <u>have</u> to go into one book.

The book will have two covers. There will be no front or back. My story will be on one side. Flip it over upside down to read Cleo's story.

"It's called a flip book," Rebecca said. "It's a perfect solution."

(Question: Is it a flip book because the authors flipped out while working on it????)

Rebecca is also forcing us to illustrate each other's stories! Isn't there a law against that? Where is my lawyer mother when I need her?

I think our flip book will be a flop. Does that make it a flip-flop book?

(New category of book? Sold with sandals in the summer?)

Rebecca said that this is the only possible solution.

HA! I can think of <u>lots</u> of others:
a) letting me work on my own book
b) pairing me and Mira
c) sending Cleo home!

<u>A Tale of Two Cousins Working</u>
<u>On One Book</u>

Scene: A kitchen table in the home of Grandma Emma, a cheerful grandmother who collects salt and pepper shakers.

It is raining outside. Zipper, a small black dog, lies on the kitchen floor.

The supper dishes have just been washed.

The two cousins sit as far away from each other as possible. Sheets of paper, pencils, and various art supplies are spread over the table.

It is tense in the room. You could cut the tension with a knife.

Question: Why a knife? Why not a scissors or a razor blade or a saw? The tension is so thick here, you'd need to cut it with an ax!

As the scene opens, the two cousins are finishing their book illustrations.

Grandma Emma (enters room): How wonderful to see you two working together!
Abby draws an ugly brown-haired cousin picking on a sweet red-haired cousin.
Cleo draws an ugly red-haired cousin picking on a sweet brown-haired cousin.
Grandma Emma: Both so creative!
Abby makes flames spout from brown-haired cousin's nose.
Cleo puts fangs on red-haired cousin.
Grandma Emma: I did the right thing bringing you together.

Abby gives brown-haired cousin gigantic knobby knees.

Cleo gives red-haired cousin warts.

Grandma Emma smiles at her granddaughters, puts on a rain slicker, and takes Zipper out for his evening walk.

Cleo turns red-haired cousin into hideous monster.

Abby makes brown-haired cousin into hideous witch.

As if it can't bear the sight of so much hideousness, the curtain suddenly falls.

After a few minutes, it rises again.

The house is silent. Two cousins draw. And draw. And draw. The drawings get uglier and uglier and uglier and uglier and uglier and uglier and uglier and uglier and UGLIER until . . .

. . . Abby screams.

Abby: <u>Enough!</u>
Cleo (scowls): Of . . . ?

Abby: You <u>know</u>.

Cleo: Oh. That.

Abby (takes breath): Please?

Cleo: Hmmm.

Abby: If you —

Cleo (quickly): Okay.

Abby: Okay??

Cleo: <u>Okay!</u>

The two girls throw down their markers. They glance at each other across the table.

Abby: Sorry, um, you know, for, uh . . .

Cleo: Yeah, I'm sorry, too.

Abby (embarrassed laugh): What were we fighting about, anyway?

Cleo: I, uh, well, I thought you were so, uh, perfect.

Abby: <u>Me???</u> It's you who's perfect!

Cleo (astonished laugh): Then why does Grandma Emma always brag about how wonderful you are?

Abby: She brags about <u>you</u>!

Cleo and Abby frown at each other.

Cleo: You're the perfect kid from the perfect family.

Abby: <u>You</u> have perfect manners and per-
fect grades!
  Cleo: I think you've got it all wrong.
  Abby: No, you do.
  Cleo: Wanna bet?
  Abby: YEAH!

The cousins seem about to fight again.
Then suddenly they begin to giggle. They
point at each other and accuse the other of
being perfect. But now everything is funny.
Once they start laughing, they can't stop.
They look at each other's hideous pictures
and laugh some more.

Chapter 11

Friday

"Miracles happen."

Fate and Destiny Calendar

They _do_.

I still can't believe it.
Are Cleo and I _really_ friends?

Rebecca placed a package of paper cups and a jug of lemonade on one of the tables.

"Bring the refreshments over here," she called to the people who were streaming into the greenhouse room.

Parents deposited bowls of fruit, pitchers of iced tea, and plates of cookies on the table. There was an urn of coffee and also hot water for tea. A few people had brought cakes, and one family had contributed a pizza.

"Here are a few more treats," Grandma Emma said, setting two plates of brownies on the table.

"Thanks," Rebecca said. "They look delicious."

Cleo grabbed Grandma Emma's arm. "Come see the books!"

"Ours is a flip book," Abby explained. "Two books in one." She placed it in Grandma Emma's hands.

"This is wonderful!" Grandma Emma said proudly.

Rebecca went to the front of the room and smiled at the assembled group. Parents, grandparents, and friends were chatting and looking at the books. A group of younger children chased one another around the room.

"Welcome to our bookmaking workshop," Rebecca announced.

The room quieted down.

"Your sons and daughters have learned so much this week — and so have I," Rebecca said. "They've produced some fine picture books that they're eager to read. As soon as everyone finds a seat, we'll get started!"

Abby scanned the room for a place to sit. Mira stood up and waved to her. She pointed to three empty chairs next to hers.

As they sat down, Mira introduced everyone to her father and brother. Her father nodded hello. Her little brother was tracing his hand on a piece of paper.

"Rebecca's wearing shoes today," Abby said.

"I think she should have come barefoot," Mira whispered back.

"Barefoot with braids," Cleo said.

It felt funny to be friends with Cleo, Abby thought. As if they *ought* to be fighting. She was glad they weren't.

When everyone had found a seat, Rebecca pointed to two boys at the back of the room. "You're our first readers!"

The boys slouched to the front of the room and picked up their book, *Howl of the Alien.*

"One night, an eerie howl shattered the peace of the planet Gorx. . . ." The boys took turns reading, handing each other the book.

"That was exciting," Rebecca said when they had finished. "What a dramatic tale!"

The audience applauded and cheered.

Mira and her partner were next. Mira stood shyly

while the other girl read the story. It was about a whisper that traveled in search of an ear.

"Very imaginative," Rebecca commented. "I love the illustrations!"

"We did a combination of collage and drawings," Mira explained in a quiet voice that could barely be heard.

"Bravo!" her father called.

"Great job!" Abby yelled.

Mira's brother waved his drawing paper like a flag. "More!" he cried.

Next came Abby and Cleo's turn. Suddenly Abby was very nervous.

She showed everyone the two covers of the book.

"Cleo and I wrote our own stories and illustrated each other's," Abby said. Her heart was racing and her face felt hot. She felt as if she could barely speak. "We'll read each other's story, too."

Abby handed the book to Cleo.

"*Cousin Confusion* by Abby Hayes, illustrated by Cleo Wayne," Cleo began. "There once lived two cousins of the same age who were as different as could be . . ."

When Cleo finished reading, there was applause and laughter. Cleo gave the book back to Abby.

"*Crazy Cousin* by Cleo Wayne, illustrated by Abby Hayes," Abby read. "Once upon a time, there lived two cousins. They lived together in a gingerbread house with their sweet old Grammy Mammy . . ."

She rushed through the story. But there was applause and laughter at the end of her reading, too.

Cleo unfolded a sheet of paper. "Wait!" she said. "We're not finished!"

"We wrote an afterword to our stories," Abby mumbled. "It's very short."

"The cousins who once couldn't stand each other lived happily ever after," Cleo and Abby read in unison.

When they returned to their seats, Grandma Emma looked thoughtful.

She smiled at both girls but didn't say anything.

"That was great," Mira said. "I loved it! The stories were like mirror images of each other."

"It was really funny," her brother added.

"How did you get the idea?" Mira's father asked.

"Real life," Abby said.

"Imagination," Cleo said.

Everyone laughed.

"A little of both?" Mira's father said.

"Did you like our book?" Abby asked Grandma Emma.

"Yes," Grandma Emma replied. "Especially the happy ending."

After everyone had read their books, the workshop participants and their guests crowded around the refreshment table.

"Congratulations on a fine job," Grandma Emma said to Rebecca. "The girls had a good week. They learned a lot."

Rebecca nodded. "I think Cleo and Abby learned more than anyone."

"Who, us?" Cleo said.

"We *did*?" Abby said.

Rebecca took a bite of one of Grandma Emma's brownies.

"Your granddaughters surprised me," she said to Grandma Emma. "I didn't think they were going to finish their book, much less read it out loud. I *never* thought they'd write an ending together!"

Cleo and Abby glanced at each other.

We surprised ourselves, Abby thought.

"Or that they'd end up as friends," Rebecca added. She looked at Abby and Cleo. "How did you do it?"

"Well, we . . . " Abby tried to find the words, but none came.

Cleo finished her thought. "Well, we . . . we thought it was funny."

"Funny?" Rebecca repeated in astonishment. "What?"

"How we, um, made each other into evil monsters," Abby said.

"Nasty, awful monsters," Cleo explained.

"With warts," Abby said.

"And knobby knees," Cleo added.

"And flame-throwing nostrils," Abby said.

They began to giggle.

"Abby and Cleo both have a sense of humor," Rebecca said to Grandma Emma. "And they did excellent work together."

"Thank you," Grandma Emma said.

"I have an idea for your next collaboration," Rebecca said to Abby and Cleo. "Why don't you write the story of how you became friends?"

"Maybe," Abby said hesitantly. She looked at Cleo.

Cleo adjusted her glasses. "We could e-mail it back and forth," she suggested.

"That'd be fun!" Abby said.

* * *

As they left the workshop, Rebecca gave each participant a copy of one of her books. She had autographed them.

"Good-bye!" Cleo and Abby said to Rebecca. "Thanks for the writing workshop! We loved it!"

"Good-bye!" Abby called to Mira. She wanted to say more, but she didn't know what. Have a nice life? Hope I see you in the future? It didn't seem likely that they'd ever meet again.

At least she and Cleo didn't hate each other anymore.

Grandma Emma unlocked the car doors. The girls slid into the backseat.

"I have to do a quick errand," Grandma Emma said. "Can I leave you two here for a moment?"

"Of course!" Cleo said.

The two girls opened their books to read what Rebecca had written.

Abby's inscription said, "I will never forget you and your cousin! Good luck with your writing!"

Cleo's inscription said, "You and Abby are unforgettable! Don't ever lose your sense of humor!"

"I have a sense of humor, too," Abby protested. "Why didn't she put that in mine?"

"And *I* like to write," Cleo said.

"Huh!" Abby said.

"Yeah!" Cleo agreed. She shut the book and sighed. "I wish we had another week with Grandma Emma and Rebecca. And Mira, too."

"I do, too," Abby said. "But I miss my family."

"My parents are always giving lectures and attending conferences," Cleo said. "They're always on the road. I wish I had a nice, normal family like yours."

"Nice? Normal?" Abby repeated. "You should spend a week with the Twin Tornados."

"The Twin Tornados? Your sisters? Aren't they superstars?"

"Superstar fighters!!" Abby said. "Superstar bossy!"

Cleo nodded as if she understood. "I'd hate that. But I don't like being an only child. It gets lonely."

"That's what my best friend, Jessica, said. She's an only child, too. But now she's living with her father and stepfamily." Abby found herself telling Cleo all about Jessica and her long stay in Oregon.

"It must be hard to lose your best friend," Cleo said. "But I wish I had an instant family like Jessica."

"I'll share *my* family with you," Abby offered. "If you can stand my sisters."

Chapter 12

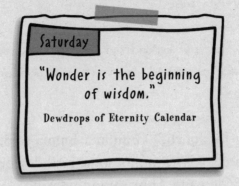

Saturday

"Wonder is the beginning of wisdom."

Dewdrops of Eternity Calendar

<u>Abby's wonder list</u>:

1. How did Cleo and I go from being enemies to being friends so quickly?
2. Why were we enemies at all?
3. How did I miss it? Cleo is <u>really</u> great!
4. Why did she dislike me? (She now thinks I'm great, too!)
5. Why did we waste almost the whole week fighting??
6. How much fun would we have had if we'd been friends from the start?

That is a lot of wondering! I must be getting very wise.

Today is my birthday! Hooray! Grandma Emma has promised to take us shopping this morning!

"It's time for lunch," Grandma Emma said, looking at her watch. "Who wants some birthday pizza?"

"Me!" Cleo and Abby said in unison.

They had shopped for the last three hours. Abby had two new calendars from Grandma Emma. She also had a new purple purse and a set of purple barrettes. Alex, Eva, and Isabel had sent her a gift certificate for a stationery store. She had bought rainbow envelopes and a set of gel pens.

"See?" Cleo said. "It's great to have sisters and a brother."

"*Some*times," Abby said.

With her own money, Abby had bought a miniature notebook key chain. It was a real notebook with actual pages.

"Although it's so small I'd have to be a Borrower to write in it," Abby said.

"I read those books!" Cleo cried. "They're great!"

"I wish Borrowers really existed," Abby said. "Wouldn't it be amazing if there were tiny people living in our houses?"

"We could send them messages," Cleo said. "Or take them to school in our pockets."

"They'd help with math homework," Abby said.

Grandma Emma held open the door of the pizza place. "Right this way, girls." She led them to the back.

A familiar person was sitting at a table, talking to the waitress.

The table was covered with brightly wrapped packages. Balloons were tied to the chairs.

"Mira!" Abby cried.

"Why is she here?" Cleo asked.

"It must be a party," Grandma Emma said.

Mira stood up. She had a huge smile on her face. "Happy birthday, Abby!" she said.

"Happy birthday!" Cleo cried. "Surprise!"

Grandma Emma took a camera out of her bag and quickly snapped a picture. "Happy birthday to a wonderful granddaughter!" she said.

Abby couldn't catch her breath.

"Grandma Emma arranged everything yesterday after the author's tea," Cleo said. "While you and I were waiting in the car."

Grandma Emma lowered her camera. "Cleo told me who to invite."

"Me!" Mira said.

"Are you surprised?" Cleo asked.

Abby nodded. She still couldn't say a word.

"What will the birthday girl have for lunch?" Grandma Emma asked. "Aside from pizza, of course."

"A root beer float," Abby said. "And a side order of mozzarella sticks."

"Mira?" Grandma Emma said.

"May I please have a chocolate milk shake?" Mira asked.

"Lemonade for me," Cleo said. "And french fries."

As they waited for their lunch, Abby sighed with happiness. Could things get any better?

"You should have seen the look on your face when Mira said happy birthday," Cleo told Abby.

Grandma Emma pointed to the camera. "I have

the picture right here." She stood up to snap more photos of the three girls.

Mira slid a brightly wrapped gift toward her. "Don't forget your presents."

Abby picked up the package. "What is it?" she asked. "Animal, vegetable, or mineral?"

"Open it!" Cleo urged.

It was a stationery set. Some of the envelopes were addressed with Mira's name, street and number, city, state, and zip code.

"I hope you'll write me," Mira said shyly. She looked down at the table. "We could even visit sometime."

"Yes!" Abby cried. "I hope we do!"

Mira looked pleased.

"Now mine!" Cleo said, handing her a flat package wrapped in purple paper.

"You got me a present?"

Cleo looked embarrassed. "Sure," she mumbled. "Why not?"

Abby carefully unwrapped it. It was a brand-new purple notebook.

"I *love* it!" Abby cried.

"You write so much," Cleo said. "I thought you'd need a new notebook soon. It was either that or a laptop," she added with a smile.

Abby wanted to hug Cleo, but she hesitated. Wasn't it only a few days ago that they had hated each other?

Suddenly, she jumped up and threw her arms around her cousin. "This is one of the best birthdays ever!"

Chapter 13

Sunday morning

"All good things must come
to an end."

Circles and Spirals Calendar

<u>Must</u> they??

(<u>Mostly*) good things that
have come to an end:</u>
1. Flew on airplane by myself
2. Met Cleo
3. Hated Cleo (*not one of good things)
4. Attended arts program with Cleo
5. Wrote and illustrated story
6. Stopped hating Cleo
7. Made friends with Mira
8. Read book at author's tea
9. Became friends with Cleo

10. Had surprise birthday party with
    Grandma Emma, Mira, and Cleo

The events of last week could fill an entire year. But they passed like a minute.

  <u>I can't believe the week is over! I wish
it would last forever!!!</u>

Boo-hoo! Boo-hoo! <u>BOO-HOO!!!</u>

I didn't get to know Cleo well enough.
        I want to read her novel and
     talk to her about writing.
        I want to hear all about her act-
     ing. I bet she's better than Brianna!
        (And if I could learn more
        about Mira, too, that'd be great!
I hope she and I can plan a visit <u>soon!</u>)

A Novel
By Cleo Wayne

Dressed in Grandma Emma's old blue bathrobe, Cleo
came into the room she and Abby shared. She had an
orange towel wrapped around her head. She smelled
like shampoo and Grandma Emma's lavender soap.
   "Stop writing and start packing," she said to

Abby. "Grandma Emma is taking me to the bus station in forty-five minutes. Then she's taking you to the airport."

"I'm already packed," Abby said. "Are you going like that? Bathrobe and towel?"

"I wish," Cleo smiled. "All I need is my slippers."

She hauled her old green suitcase up from the floor and opened it.

Abby shut her journal and leaned back against the pillow. "Remember the first night we were here?" she asked. "You stuffed all your clothes into the drawer so you'd be the first one unpacked. I was so mad!"

Cleo put on a pair of striped shorts and a tank top. "You always beat me to the shower. I hated that."

"Years of practice with two older sisters," Abby said with a smirk.

"Don't be so smug about it!" Cleo cried, throwing a pillow at her.

Abby threw it back. "Smug? *Me?* You write your journal on a laptop!"

"I'll trade my laptop for your sisters!" Cleo said.

"It's a deal!" Abby replied.

The girls began to giggle.

Grandma Emma knocked at the door. "Twenty minutes!" she announced.

* * *

Grandma Emma, Cleo, and Abby sat on a bench in the bus station.

"Write your address and phone number in the back of my journal," Abby said to Cleo. "And your e-mail, of course." She handed her journal to her cousin. A piece of paper fluttered to the floor.

"Is that a love letter from your *friend* Casey?" Cleo teased.

Abby made a face. "Ugh! No!" She stooped to pick the piece of paper up. "It's the travel fortunes I wrote in Ms. Bunder's class before spring break."

"Travel fortunes?" Cleo repeated.

Abby unfolded the paper. "Great things come to those who travel," she read. "Travel will reunite old friends and relatives.

"Long trips are lucky.

"A mysterious cousin will change your life."

"Am I the mysterious cousin?" Cleo asked eagerly. Abby nodded.

"It sounds like your fortunes came true," Grandma Emma commented.

"The trip *was* lucky," Cleo said. "Wasn't it?"

"Yes!" Abby cried.

The bus pulled into the terminal.

"Do you have your ticket?" Grandma Emma asked Cleo. "And the snacks and drinks? And money in case of emergency?"

Cleo nodded. "Yes."

Grandma Emma hugged Cleo good-bye.

Abby tore a sheet of paper from her journal, wrote a few words, and handed it to Cleo. "A good-bye fortune for you!"

" 'The unknown beckons,' " Cleo read. She flung out her arms dramatically. "The unknown is calling me!"

"I'll call you, too," Abby said. "And don't forget about the book we're going to write together."

Abby and Cleo threw their arms around each other. Cleo picked up her suitcase and got in line. She gave the bus driver her ticket and climbed onto the bus.

Grandma Emma and Abby stood just outside airport security.

"I'm going to miss you and Cleo," Grandma Emma said. "It's been a wonderful week."

"I loved it," Abby said. "Well, most of it, anyway."

"I'm happy that you and Cleo are friends," her grandmother said.

"We almost weren't," Abby said.

Her grandmother smiled. "But you are now."

Abby hugged her grandmother. "Thanks for everything. Thanks for the arts program, and the surprise party, and the calendars, and the pancakes, and for having me."

"Good-bye!" Her grandmother waved as Abby passed through the security checkpoint. "I love you!"

The plane had taken off and was cruising above the clouds.

Abby opened her backpack. She had packed a bottle of water, a package of Grandma Emma's brownies wrapped in foil, the stationery that Mira had given her, gel pens, and her new and old purple journals.

What would it be like going home?

She was a new person now. She had made new friends and had had new experiences.

Would her family know that she had changed? Would her friends?

Would Abby want to spend more time with Natalie and Bethany? Would she want to hang around with Casey and the boys? Or would she spend time with someone new?

She didn't know. The travel fortune she had given to Cleo applied to *her*, too.

"The unknown beckons," Abby said. She opened her new purple journal, took out a pen, and began to write.

TWITCHES

Imagine finding out you have an identical twin. Cam and Alex just did. Think nothing can top that? Guess again. (They also just learned they're witches.)

In a family of superstars, it's hard to stand out. But Abby is about to surprise her friends, her family, and most of all, herself!

Heartland™

Nestled in the foothills of Virginia, there's a place where horses come when they are hurt. Amy, Ty, and everyone at Heartland work together to heal the horses—and form lasting bonds that will touch your heart.

Learn more at www.scholastic.com/books

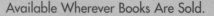

Available Wherever Books Are Sold.

■ **SCHOLASTIC**

GIRLT503